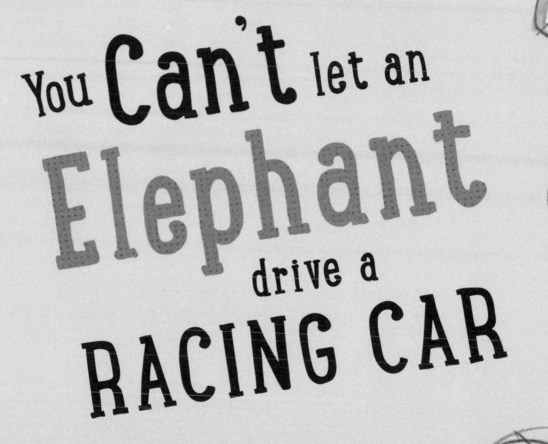

You Can't let an Elephant drive a RACING CAR

Patricia Cleveland-Peck

Illustrated by

David Tazzyman

BLOOMSBURY
CHILDREN'S BOOKS

LONDON OXFORD NEW YORK NEW DELHI SYDNEY

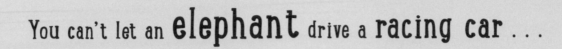

You can't let an **elephant** drive a **racing car** ...

He dreams of becoming a Grand Prix star,
but before he even gets to the start
his super-fast car starts falling apart.

Nor should you allow that young alligator

to take part in a contest for best figure-skater . . .

She'd do a HUGE loop and spin around twice,

then lose control

and skate right off the ice.

It really would be a terrible shame
to let a **kangaroo** ruin the **cricket** game . . .

She'd hit the ball HARD but let go of the bat
which would fly to a fielder
and knock
off his
hat!

The **walrus** is setting a blistering pace
in the international **bicycle race** . . .

But rounding a bend there's a bit of a hitch,
as he swerves and his rivals

end up

in
a

ditch.

If an **OCTOPUS** insists she wants to compete
at **ping-pong** — BEWARE!

She's tricky to beat . . .

With all those bats thwacking and balls *whizzing* past,
her opponent will need to play SUPER fast!

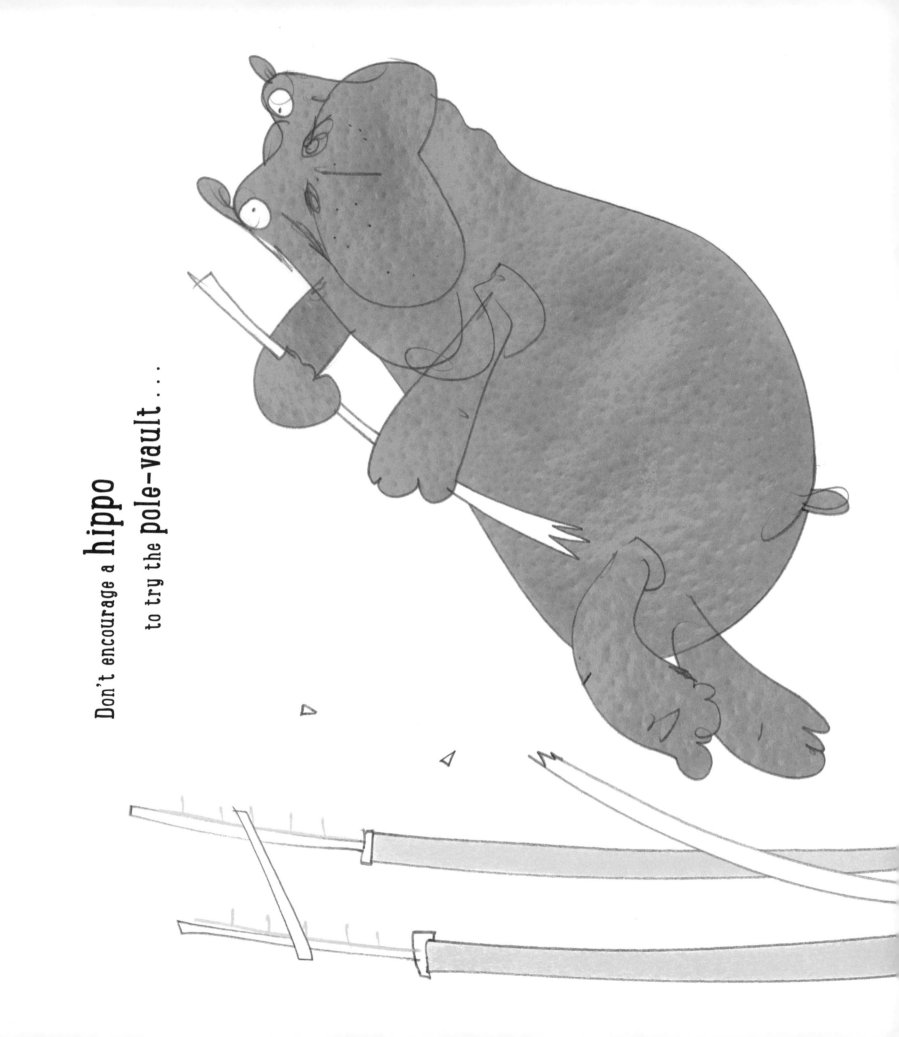

Don't encourage a **hippo**
to try the **pole-vault** . . .

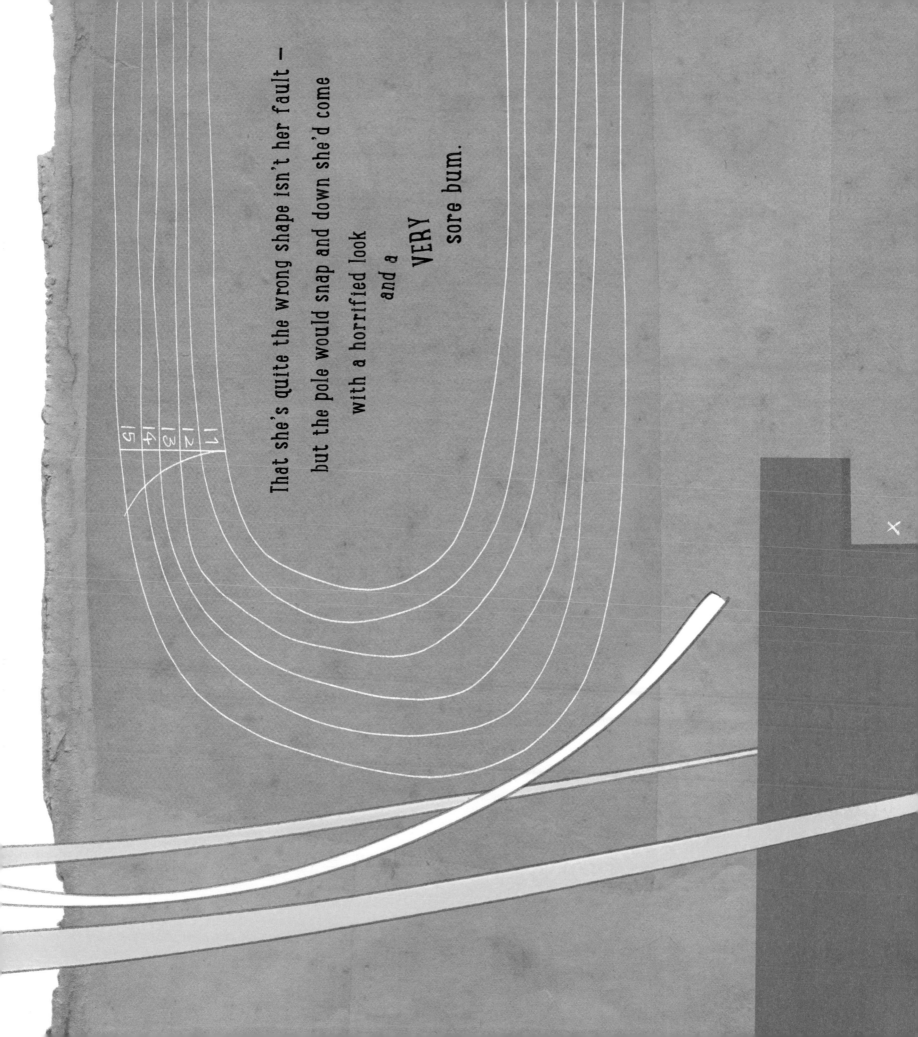

That she's quite the wrong shape isn't her fault –

but the pole would snap and down she'd come

with a horrified look

and a

VERY

sore bum.

Never partner a **stork** in a three-legged race . . .

You won't be able to keep up the pace.
And should he decide he wants to fly,
you'll find yourself upside down in the sky.

When the **wombat** tries to **lift** a **weight**
her face goes red and she gets in a state . . .

She does her BEST

but staggers and stumbles,

slips up, trips up –

and DOWN

the weight

tumbles.

Never let a **warthog** join your **football** game.

He'll bring you nothing but failure and shame . . .

He'll dig up the pitch, run off with the ball
and act in ways not sporting at all.

The swanky **puma** thinks he'll look cool
if he takes a high **dive** right into the pool . . .

But glancing down, he feels giddy and sick
and cries out,
"HELP!
Please get me
down
quick!"

The **monkeys'** finale **gymnastic** display
is a total shambles — they just want to play . . .

Some do vaults, some do handstands,
some fall on the floor.
They're having FUN —
and just look at that **score!**

"We didn't win any medals,"
the animals sigh.
"But we did our best,
we really did TRY."

There's no need to worry, never lose **heart**.
The **important** thing
is just TAKING PART.
So why not **wash away**
all your
troubles . . .

In a GIANT hot tub
full of BUBBLES!

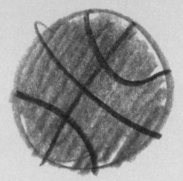

To Perry, my eldest son
with love — PC-P

To the cricketing gentlemen of the
South London Odd Balls (SLOBs) — DT

BLOOMSBURY CHILDREN'S BOOKS
Bloomsbury Publishing Plc
50 Bedford Square, London WC1B 3DP, UK
29 Earlsfort Terrace, Dublin 2, Ireland

BLOOMSBURY, BLOOMSBURY CHILDREN'S BOOKS and the Diana logo are trademarks of Bloomsbury Publishing Plc

First published in Great Britain in 2022 by Bloomsbury Publishing Plc

Text copyright © Patricia Cleveland-Peck 2022
Illustrations copyright © David Tazzyman 2022

Patricia Cleveland-Peck and David Tazzyman have asserted their rights under the Copyright, Designs and Patents Act, 1988,
to be identified as the Author and Illustrator of this work

A catalogue record for this book is available from the British Library

ISBN HB: 978 1 5266 3539 6
ISBN PB: 978 1 5266 3540 2
ISBN eBook: 978 1 5266 3541 9

1 3 5 7 9 10 8 6 4 2

Printed in Italy by L.E.G.O. S.P.A.

To find out more about our authors and books visit www.bloomsbury.com and sign up for our newsletters

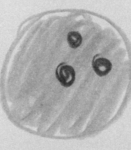